Cheryl Tomlin and Manjinder Virk have been good friends for 12 years. They worked in a pathology laboratory (virology and microbiology) together and formed a long lasting and special friendship. They are natural story tellers and are able to hold an audience through their genuinely funny sense of humour and natural story-telling aptitude. They both share an interest in writing engaging stories, utilising real life experiences as well as the supernatural.

My dear husband, David Tomlin, for supporting me.
Billy Whiting, thank you for the photo cover.
Michelle Wallis.
Nick De Silva.

Love Cheryl x

My dear family and friends, thank you so much for everything always.

Love,
Manjinder
x

Cheryl Tomlin and
Manjinder Virk

15:37

AUSTIN MACAULEY PUBLISHERS™
LONDON • CAMBRIDGE • NEW YORK • SHARJAH

A CIP catalogue record for this title is available from the British Library.

ISBN 9781398423299 (Paperback)
ISBN 9781398423305 (ePub e-book)

www.austinmacauley.com

First Published 2022
Austin Macauley Publishers Ltd®
1 Canada Square
Canary Wharf
London
E14 5AA

Thanks to Austin Macauley Publishers.

This is only the beginning for SM Skully.

Prologue

Dear Jake, I love you more than I can describe. I know you're tiny, but you're my whole world. My world is hectic, baby; Mummy's a writer; she'll spend all day on this bright shiny thing with an apple on it, and you'll want to have a go, I know. Just one piece of advice, baby, always plug in the charger. Now back to my point. Nana loves you so much, as does Granddad. He can't wait to take you to play catch, fish and all the things a little boy would do with his dad…

I know, one day you will want to know about him, I just hope that day doesn't come…

Love,
Mummy
xxxx

Chapter 1

We have all had those friends who are our lives; it's almost obsessive how much time you spend together. Every day, until you force yourself away from your phone to sleep. Then there are those who drift away as we grow older, make new friends and date.

Not these guys though. These guys spent all their lives with each other; almost bonded in their obsession to be friends forever, each year a pact, each year a celebration and each year they grew older and closer. Every day, they would walk to school together, they were on and off the bus together; homework, prom, dating; they were each other's lives.

Humidity lightly lingered in the air, as the sun was beginning to set. They stood back to back in a circle so close they could hear each other's heartbeat, and according to Jess, hear each other's thoughts—she's such a girl. They had all grown up together in the same neighbourhood. They went to the same school, dined at the same diner since preschool. Their families were all friends and spent Christmas's, birthdays and thanksgivings together. In and out of each other's homes, they would come and go, sitting for hours talking about life, drinking, smoking, laughing and sharing their most intimate secrets with each other. No one could break their circle of friendship; nobody got that close.

The rule of karma appears in life, balance always has to be restored in the cosmos. Too much of a good thing tends not to last, and this was the best thing.

Each year, their pact to have each other's back was written on a piece of paper and tied to the tree outside the school grounds behind the janitor's shed. No one came there since the janitor had left years before.

The school was an old private school that looked like Hogwarts had had a designer baby. The ceilings were high and walls made of stone, but the stark art on the walls were impressionist and abstract. Dean was convinced the pictures were nudes which the principal had brought and defaced during his mid-life crisis. He spent a lot of time talking and trying to convince the others of this. Mark humoured him and used a marker pen to deface the one hanging in the main reception, one random day. Mark was always up for a dare, Danny not so much.

Danny was the sweetest. All the girls rallied around him for a cuddle and his soft nature. His smile was bright and voice deep. He made them laugh when he spoke.

Dean was strong with floppy hair covering his eyes. He was tall, oldest by a month and the quietest, but wise like a wizard, Joe would say. Dean was not great at school; average, if average was a thing. He never wanted to be there. His dreams were bigger than the small town. He was going to play football for the majors and be the youngest quarterback the world had ever seen. The books he carried were used to prop up his running shoes. Girls would hover around him but his great loves were football and her. Only she could get him to listen on her say, so he'd do anything.

Jess was naturally beautiful, not that any of them noticed or she would let them. Dungarees all the time and a football under her arm.

Mark was the dad. He had hit puberty first and had shot up in height. His voice was deep, and he looked strong. The guys would compare guns at every opportunity; it was always a case of suns out guns out. Mark was the tallest and looked older than his years. His growth spurt meant he towered at six feet over his classmates. He would be the one that brought booze to the parties, bought weed and could drive. His blond hair swept across one side of his face and held back when he ran his fingers through it. The ladies loved him. His strength was obvious. He was aggressive when he was in the court, and when his friends needed him. He knew he drew all the eyes to him; he played on it. It was fun to have the Hollywood smile.

I sat there looking at the pictures I had left. If only I could go back to them, instead darkness shaded my smile. Looking so hard at the photograph, staring at his face. How could he?

Chapter 2

The blinding noise from the sirens drowned out everything on that day. There was a nervousness in the air. The curfew had been imposed, but they knew they had to meet at the usual spot. This was the system; they had each other's back in the literal sense.

They stood like this for moments, minutes felt like hours waiting for the others to turn up—they had to check if they were all OK…The trees lined the streets, and the lawns were so neat it was almost unbelievable. Everything was green and bright, but dark clouds were closing in.

The code: "What were you doing at 15:37 today?" Jess asked suspiciously, eyeing up her life brothers. She smiled with her eyes.

"I was at the mall," Mark said.

Only one answer from the four boys.

No one spoke for moments; it was so quiet. Even the smallest of the insects could be heard. There were grasshoppers jumping from their newly evicted premises to the nearest hedges.

"Can I speak to you, Joe?" Dean, the eldest of the five, the tallest and biggest said.

Silence…

“Can I speak to you, Joe?” he asked again, his voice quivering, his eyes wild and pupils dilated like a captured animal.

Joe did not speak. He moved quickly, snarling.

Jess felt herself melt, her body becoming weak. The football under her arm fell to the ground and rolled away. Something was wrong.

Four hearts beating in unison tightened with fear. The fifth had lost its beat.

Screams echoed between the trees, as Mark and Danny ran, not looking back, running away from the horror that no young innocent eyes should see.

Jess screamed with horror as she ran…she turned for a moment and saw Joe frozen, he had not moved. The setting sun obscuring her vision as forming tears glistened in her eyes. She gulped deep breaths, and she ran, trying to pick up the pace but her fragile frame was failing her. Something is wrong with Joe.

She shouts, ‘Joe, are you ok?’

She didn’t see him move an inch until he was there. She had pain in her sides, the air felt heavy in her lungs as she fought fear and panic. The adrenaline was making her heart feel like it was trying to escape. She stopped to catch her breath, leaning on the wall as the world became blurry. The wall was cold and wet from fresh paint. Her breathing too laboured to scream as she felt the cold hand on her shoulder. The tears streamed down her cheek. He had her.

Tight up against the wall, Joe had Jess tearing at her; frenzied, trying to separate the flesh to satisfy his hunger. The world quickly became dark. The noise was like nothing that they had heard before; it echoed between the homes. The boys could hear it, but not understand what was beginning.

This was followed by complete silence. No birds, grasshoppers or animals could be heard, for that quick sudden terrifying moment, time had stood still.

Danny and Dean stood side by side, staring into oblivion. Not quite absorbing what had happened. Mark paced quickly behind them, trying to clear his head. He was speaking, shouting maybe, but the screams in the mind of Mark were blocking all sounds. What had they seen? What had happened to Joe? Where was Jess?

Mark struggled to catch his breath; struggled to speak or understand what had happened. They'd made their way to their safe spot; it was instinctive that they had not gone anywhere else. What the hell had just happened?

"Dean, what were you going to ask Joe?" Mark grabbed him by the collar, forgetting his own strength. Dean squirmed and fell to the ground as Mark let go.

Danny was pacing. They were to meet here should something like this happen! They had prepared; all of them. It was minutes before they realised Jess was not there. Rage built up in Danny. A loud scream echoed in the space, "How could we let this happen? Jess!" they cried.

Dean slumped on the floor and let out a whisper, "He's a monster, I've seen his eyes. She's dead."

Mark opened the door, the handle had janitor written all over it. The 'do not enter' sign fell with the force he used. He sat down on the wet grass, head in his hands, looking up to the sky, he questioned everything that had happened, should he go back? The pact said not to. Why had this happened? A single tear rolled down his strong-featured face.

Still feeling hungry, Joe walked slowly away from his appetiser. His dark grey hoodie covering his head, hands in his pockets. His medium frame casting a large shadow; the sun burned. He had never noticed it before as he walked. He liked that he was not on his own. He tried to dodge it, and run away from it. He chuckled and thought it was amusing.

The sun was at its fullest, glowing with a menacing aura, taunting him; he scowled as he looked for his next prey. He didn't know where he was going; the curving path felt like it went on forever. His jeans had been torn and his trainers felt wet. The path took him to the lake with a big house on the corner. It was lovely. The blue of the lake with the sun casting shadows from the weeping willows; he was not sure if he had sensed it before he heard it, but something caught his attention. He turned his head slightly. His hoody moved to one side, exposing his prominent features, his sharp nose deep set with black empty unseeing unfeeling eyes and a tuft of blond fringe mixed with a pale complexion. The sun exposed the terror within; the rays hit him, bouncing off his body, spurring him on.

The house was big; too big. The glass from the bay windows glistened as the sun hit them, encased in their brick prison. The big heavy wooden front door creaked as Edie opened it. He caught a glimpse of her, which framed her in his mind as a tall, slim built and good-looking women with dark hair, greying in places. Good for her age. Edie was 50 years old but looked a lot younger. She kept herself in good shape and had a lot of admirers. Dinners were always a mix of glitz and flirting, hence the dinner parties were very successful.

Edie walked down the path, holding the remains of yesterday's dinner party. The bag was as heavy as her head felt. She saw no one,-just the trees rustling as always. Feeling happy, she started walking to end of the path. She heard or saw nothing. Still thinking about last night and what a success it was, her promotion to CEO for the company she worked for. She smiled to herself, proud she had reached a stage in her life where everything was just perfect.

Joe smirked, almost a laugh which turned into a hoarse cackle, waiting for the crucial moment. Playing, hiding, dodging in and out of the bushes and trees, then without warning, he pounced on her, dragging her down. She fell on her stomach.

Edie was startled she was on the floor. She didn't know what was happening to her. Then the pain hit her like a lightning bolt; it was unbearable. She wished for death to come quickly, but it never came. He took his time; her hot blood pouring from her punctured veins, and then she felt nothing but a sense of peace and calm.

The screams were silent and the pain intense, tearing at her calves as he dragged her towards him. He was already there before she could react; there was no escape. He found he didn't need to run to her, time would slow down for him in fear like everything else did.

Then quiet…

Chapter 3

"It's too late to help Jess, we need to help Joe," whispered Danny. They hadn't moved for a while, grief was debilitating. "We need to help him," said Danny, slightly louder this time. Dean and Mark were lost. How had this happened? Our family torn apart by our own life brother. They searched around the shed. The janitor had left some tools which were now caked in rust and cobwebs. The dust had settled on the shelves but they'd never noticed. The floor was covered in cushions, cushions Jess had brought to sit on. Mark walked towards the tools, throwing each to a side with force, frantically searching for something.

Dean and Danny watched as a cloud of dust filled the room, and as it cleared, Mark was standing, dishevelled, not himself. Mark was holding a box, and the box was heavy. The gun the janitor had left; his hands shook holding it. They had vowed never to hurt each other. A raindrop fell into a puddle formed next to the door, breaking his train of thought.

He could hear Danny, helplessness washed over him. "How…? How do we help him?" Dean was fighting his rage; it was a deep heat that he found hard to control. He clenched his fist at the thought of Jess and Joe; he had turned whilst running. Joe had grabbed her, lifting her from the ground. He had seen Joe's eyes, they were red like blood, and his mouth was foaming.

Mark looked up. "He's too far gone…what he has done is unforgiveable…he killed her!" he shouted.

"Maybe she's OK," Danny said meekly. Danny was always the kindest, the one with hope.

Dean knew she wasn't, he'd seen her fall; the life had fallen from her beautiful green eyes. In the sun they looked hazel, her face a vision of beauty, her hair gold, silky and soft. He felt a sharp stab in his chest. She was gone and he could never tell her about his feelings for her; loving her, breathing her since they were children. The pain hurt, his heart broken, he saw her killed by his own life brother. Two people he loved and adored; two precious lives taken.

"Maybe the police can help." Danny let out before holding his head in his hands.

"We can't call them, what if he hasn't done anything. They'll send him back inside."

They just stared at each other. They had all the trust in the world, but not in him. Joe had always been a bit rogue. He came to them later in middle school, but he felt like family. He didn't have much, but he wanted more. So much so that he had tried to take it.

Chapter 4

I am Him.

I walked almost gliding. Each step felt lighter than ever, something was drawing me there. Everything appeared sharper, more vivid. Birds were singing, the grass was greener, and I felt strong. My strength could keep me walking to the end of the earth.

I found my way to a gated building, the old asylum secured by walls and hedges. We'd been scared of this place. Every Halloween, we'd run past daring each other inside. It was heavily guarded. Security to keep the world's most dangerous predators in, or was it to keep them out? I can't help but laugh out loud. The five of us used to stand outside, waiting to see if we could see anyone. I think we would have died if they had come up to the fence, just memories of past life, a life I used to have, a life that was mine and not whatever was running through my blood, oozing out from my pores. I keep walking, not tired, just focused.

A sound disturbed my thoughts before I realise where I am, I hid against the greenery, excited, hungry, heart beating so fast it hurt against my chest, beating on my ribs, my lips dried and cracked, it hurt but I didn't care; all I wanted was to taste the wonderful, glorious blood from the young ones.

Their blood is sweeter and not that thick, so it goes down a lot quicker. I laugh a demonic evil laugh, it comes from inside.

I fear myself, but have to be quiet, so I must be careful not to make a sound. He is young, blond and alert. He looks my way and my eyes bulge so wide, it hurts. He turned as his name was called. "Mark!" It was Danny, followed behind him was Dean. They called him inside.

They'd made it here. A familiar sense of relief dimmed by a new indescribable feeling—they were OK, but for how long? The rustling disturbed me. I couldn't stop the noise, stupid nature! I can wait; I have waited a long time to fulfil my desires.

The asylum had two turrets holding telescopes, like binoculars protecting this fortress, big spot lights lit up the area. It was getting dark and cold, perfect for the hunt. I pulled my hood up, hunger growled within me—it was loud, thc feeling intensified—Did they know I was there?—How? Did they know what I had done to Edie? The pain inside was too much—JESS—what have I done? My best friend; it was all too much; the anger, pain. I rushed out of the bushes with a vengeance, with hatred and—love, feelings I thought I would never feel again.

Then nothing.

The smell of fresh blood filled my nostrils; I needed to feed. The pain in my chest made me stop, it was an intense fiery feeling of sinking—drowning. Voices of my best friends in the distance. Mark, Dean, Danny crying and shouting; my friends and my brothers asking, "What have you done?"

My chest felt heavy. I reached to soothe the pain, and blood was pouring out like rain. They had shot me.

The voices of my three lifelong best friends were loud at first, and then it faded.

Chapter 5

"What were you doing at 15:37 today?"

My mum, Olivia, was in the kitchen washing up the lunch dishes, singing to herself with a slight contented smile on her face. She was a good-looking woman for her 45 years. Her skin was pale and her eyes blue. Her blonde hair complimented her freckles. Mum had a mild temperament when she met my father at a barn dance. She always said that he had two left feet and Dad, he always laughed it off.

My dad, Elliott, was five years older than Mum, standing six feet in height; a robust man with large hands, but a gentle giant with light wispy blond hair. At 50 years old, Dad could give a 20-year-old a run for their money. He was in the front room, watching football; shouting and cheering. They couldn't have any more children after me, so I was an only child, but not really, as I had my life brothers and sister.

As the heat was unbearable, I wandered outside. The atmosphere was as humid and sticky as in the house. Funny, no sound anywhere, so quiet and peaceful, like something was coming, a feeling or premonition?

A slight noise made me turn towards the barn; the sound was coming from inside. Usually I'd leave it, natural curiosity wasn't within me—I walked towards it, exploring my surroundings with my eyes. Nothing different, same junk cluttered the fields, then the rustling—it was moving. I saw a glimpse of what looked like a large dog; foaming at the mouth, a rabid dog. I shouted. No sound came out of my mouth; just silence. He circled me once, twice. He stopped and sniffed the air. His stare was hypnotising, nothing but darkness in his eyes; he growled—too late. My legs were too heavy to run, he pounced. My eyes closed instinctively, maybe if I can't see him, he will go away—I felt myself fall. I was down on the floor struggling to breathe—to live.

I couldn't breathe; it hurt. Shivering, clenching my jaw so tight. I was afraid to open my eyes. There was blood everywhere on my clothes. I could feel it pouring like water. I was torn. I couldn't focus properly.

I couldn't see the dog. Was I alright? I winced in pain as I got up. There was a deep laceration on my arm. Time blinked on the dial of my watch; 15:37. I fixated momentarily. The blood began to stain the dial.

"Where is the dog?" I get up and hear nothing. What to do? What to do? Mum, Dad?—I needed to keep them safe. I sat and tore a strip of my shirt to stop the bleeding. I felt the need to lie down. I needed to think. This went through my mind as I arose to stagger towards home. Why did the heat bother me so much. If only I had just stayed with Dad. I reached the porch; the warm light glows from the television, I could see Mum walking towards Dad, laying her hand on his shoulder. He was asleep. I looked down; a trail of blood from the field to the porch. I couldn't do this to them, "I love you, Mum. I love you, Dad," escapes my mouth, as I turn to walk away.

I needed to see my friends if only to say goodbye. I heard them before they see me they are saying something about dead bodies and a rabid—a rabid what? “The dog that attacked me?” I couldn’t hear, and my head was thumping, I grabbed my arm.

My blood was rushing around my head, I couldn’t understand. Lots of questions, lots of talking, too much noise. I’d say nothing if they ask about my injury. I will tell them I fell. Only I know the truth. They look at me with questionable eyes, before we turn back-to-back…I close my eyes, thinking I should have told them. Why didn’t I tell them???

The feeling of dread, a knot in my stomach, what will become of me?

“Where were you at 15:37?”

If they ask again, I will tell them, this is where I was at 15:37. This is what happened to me at 15:37.

Staring up at the ceiling, I thought of my brothers. What were they doing and would they forgive me? I need to find them to tell them how sorry I am, to beg for forgiveness, to see Jess’s grave, lay flowers and cry for the friend I will never see again. To hold her and tell her how I loved her then and always will do.

I want to ask Edie’s family for forgiveness and to try and put the past behind us all. To take Sophie in my arms so that I can smell her clean fresh hair and hope she sees the good in me, and to let me show her how sorry I am.

They’re taunting me; the memories. Everyone is close enough to touch, but disappear as I reach them. I miss them, whoever these figures are. There are so many people, backpackers, women and Mum.

Chapter 6

I close my eyes for a little while and dream. Friends, family and terror are what my dreams are made of; a lot of jumbled bits of memories.

The sun is setting as we set off for home. I feel unusually tired but needed to keep awake to feel Sophie's fear, that is what keeps me alive. The conversation is always dry in the car. She likes to drive in silence but I don't care. I have my own thoughts which are more important.

I AM FREE.

15:37! What was it about that number? A memory, a thought or a time in my life where something terrible happened. But why couldn't I remember? I feel a jolt as the car goes over a bump. I feel anger build up in me. I feel a snarl and bile rising up into my throat; it burns. I grip the sides as I try to contain my anger.

I breathe, almost gasping, fighting to catch my breath again. I calm down and close my eyes again. The moon was full as we reached our destination. Sophie hurried us in. She was still keeping her distance. I wanted to laugh but kept it in. This time, I shall leave it.

15:37, I have flash backs, memories of tragedy and pain of friends of long ago. My family, my forever; the night draws in, and I feel my chest tighten. The throbbing in my head won't go away. It pounds against my skull gnawing at me. It hurts my eyes, as I walk to the bathroom to splash water on my face. "Where's the migraine medicine, Sop?"

She doesn't hear me; instead, I slam my head into the utility cabinet.

"What happened?" she heard that.

"Nothing, just need the migraine meds quickly," I was almost screaming.

"Bathroom cabinet next to your toothbrush," she shouted.

I frantically searched for the bottle, feeling a hysteria rising within me. I don't care that everything has fallen from the shelves into the sink. The towels are on the floor as I shake the bottle into my mouth. Relief is seldom immediate. It takes minutes before a wave engulfs me, filling me with calm and tiredness, like I'd been knocked out.

I glance up at the mirror momentarily as I try to rebuild the destruction I had caused. It was not me, that boy in the mirror. There's a younger boy, he is full of freedom, not a care in the world. His eyes seem bright and innocent. The older version of me soon returns; tired lines around my eyes, a few grey hair with thin spindly veins along my forehead.

I hear a noise and turn quickly. It's Sophie, she's stunning. She stands in the guest bedroom doorway, hands clenched together in fear. Her eyes asking me if everything is OK. She's amazing, my own gazelle. Blood starts pumping, running through my body so hard that I can hear it. I breathe in quickly, and try to walk past her. As I do, she staggers. Her body pushes into the doorway. "Sorry Soph." I walk over to her and hold out my hand to balance her. She hesitates as she looks down at her hand—it is bleeding. She pulls away and stands up and walks away; her hand cupped around the wound. I smell the blood and my nostrils flare. It's delicious. I shake my head once, then twice, to get the smell away from me.

I grab my jacket from the stairwell and run. The night is clear and the air is fresh. The stars mock me and my weakness. Their bright shining bodies pointing and staring at me. The moon was bright, bearing down on me, heavy like a lead weight. Leave her alone, they say, she is pure and good, and you are made of pure evil. My shoulders fall as my head hangs low. I feel low as I trudge along. It's so quiet; the leaves aren't even crunching under my feet. I'm focused on the trail in front of me until something moves. My face moves into a grin and crouch to move in closer to see what it is. I clear the leaves back and see nothing. I can smell something as I search more frantically. She's tiny when I finally see her. A tiny kitten wandering beneath the thistles. I pick her up in one quick swoop, all white and fluffy with one pink eye and one blue eye. It's fascinating. She snuggles into my chest. she is warm, and I can feel her heart.

I wake up in bed alone with my thoughts. I can't remember much. I got home last night and my mouth felt dry. What did I do last night? Sophie's already awake by now, as I reach to check my phone. The case is sticky, and there's a trail of mud that I must've trekked in on the floor. Sophie must be so mad. I'll clean it. I push my legs off the bed, and my feet thud on the floor. I hear loud voices at the front of the house; a child's piercing cry so high pitched, it hurts my ears. I leap off the bed.

What on earth? I stop dead as I see a little girl with a ball of red wool in her hands crying at the end of the drive. Her clothes seemed to be covered in red paint? People gathering around, she has tears running down her pretty freckled cheeks with eyes red. What had happened?

Sophie turns and looks at me. No, she looks through me. Her eyes were cold. "What have you done?" she asks. Her sadness invades my head and my heart. It couldn't be me.

I feel nothing.

The woods are a release for me. I lie down under the trees and look up into the clear blue sky through the trees. There is a light breeze as I drift off. The smell wakes me up from a dreamless sleep. A familiar smell. It comes in waves filling my every pore. I can't place it. I leap up quickly, pull up my hoodie over my head and begin the hunt.

Everything is heightened. All the colours vivid and bright. There in the bushes, I stop. A girl of about 18 years old. She has her bag next to her and her hair in a ponytail. My brain flashes to something momentarily as I shake my head to clear it. I wait. I feel myself snarl; a grin, a familiar sense of deja vu. She hears me with fear in her eyes she tries to run. It's too late. I hold her up with one hand. I'm surprised by my strength; it takes no effort. I see an oak tree and see myself playing with my food.

"I know it's an oak tree as I used to collect acorns many years before under that same tree." I look at her. She is pleading, begging. I've been here before and I frown for a moment. The sound of her screaming wakes me and excites me. Then she stops screaming. I tilt me head to look at her; humans are amazing. Each one the same and yet so different. We all have the same structure but wow, some of us have beauty that is truly skin deep. I make myself laugh in hysterics as I have her face in my hands. I stand and think for a minute, grinning like a Cheshire cat. Then it hits me "JESS!"

What had I done? I don't feel her drop from my arms. I was running before I realised where I was going. I was gasping for air so hard, my lungs were burning. I managed to slump by a brook cowering like an animal. My reflection scaring me. There was blood everywhere. I had to wash the blood from my hands, arms and face, and get home. To Sophie, she was my safety, she was my home.

It's dark by the time I reach home; the stars are out. Black clouds hiding them—nature playing hide and seek. I let myself into the house quietly and walk up the stairs to the bedroom. All the lights were off. The bedroom door was locked, and I try the handle again. I feel angry as I find it won't relent. I want to break it down with one big hit. Instincts egg me on, they scream go for it, but I know that I must keep my cool. I pull myself up, compose myself and walk away.

Chapter 7

Sophie lay awake in the centre of the bed terrified; her mind running. He was not the man I had married, what had happened to him? What was he capable of? I miss him.

She could not wait until the morning to come. She sat up all night in fear that Joe might come back and break down the bedroom door.

Daylight broke through the heavy chintz curtains. I opened my eyes wide to get used to the light, blinking and closing them again. I had not slept. I dragged myself up, and staggered to the shower; scrubbing my skin so hard that it is left red and sore, cleaning away the sins I think to myself. There's noise in the kitchen. Sophie is cooking. She has her back to me. I love her so much. She doesn't know I'm up. I gravitate towards her silently and reach to grab her by the waist. Sophie let out a scream and let go of the frying pan. I miss her laugh. Her face as she turns around is filled with fear and terror; I see it in her eyes. It makes me angry, how could she fear me. I react before I know it, I can anticipate her every move as she struggles to pass me. I let her pass and she runs upstairs, me following shortly after, catching her before she can close the bedroom door.

There's poison in my veins.

I have her in my arms but not as I'd like. She's not happy but it doesn't faze me. She's mine and I want to be close to her, my nose grazes her neck, and I catch her scent.

Sophie felt confused. His arms were the safest place in the world, and now they felt the most dangerous. He held her for a second, and she did not want to struggle. It was him; her Joe. Sophie almost melted into his chest. Her eyes fixed on the space behind him, there was blood. She screamed and moved to push him away. What happened next was something that can only be described as pain, excruciating beyond anything she had ever felt before. Joe had bitten her.

I had gone too far this time, I knew it.

Why me? Why did I live?

I had to find my brothers, to explain to make things better and to find help.

I couldn't look at her, my angel; she lay perfectly still. I had to run. I could not bear to face what he had done.

Chapter 8

I needed to wake myself up! The headaches were excruciating, clawing to reality and the hunger was explosive; the ravenous feeling inside causing me to stir from this nightmare, dream or was it a vision?

I arose from the nightmare, breathing heavily with a twisted grin and teeth grinding together. She was restful as always, my wife, my darling Sophie. I run my fingers through her hair, with skin so soft. I hear the growl within me, and my hand quickly reaches across my face to fight the urge to bite.

It's not enough, I draw blood from my hand to supress the urge to taste, the smell so familiar. I hurry out of bed to the bathroom, the blood drips from my hand as I run the cold tap, and I watch it flow down the drain in circles, each drop darker than the previous. The hunger is insatiable, I need to eat. I hear her breathing gently. I can't look at her as I make my way out of the bedroom and down the stairs, quickly but quietly. "Come on, hurry up!" the need to get to the fridge, the need to look inside, missing steps as I go.

The magnets on the fridge hold my attention for a moment, photos of us held as a vigil. All red magnets. I open the fridge and the smell hits me first, Liver. I rip open the paper which covers it. It's raw and oozing blood—I am drawn to it.

The feeling is too much. I have to have it. More blood dripping over the same hand I just washed, only this is better, moreish. I won't wash my hands this time. There will be no need to as I lick them clean. The clock catches my attention. Why???

I have finished my banquet. What a feast! I feel ashamed. Ashamed of my desire not for my darling wife who sleeps peacefully waiting for my return, but for a piece of flesh from a dead animal.

I make my way back upstairs to the bedroom, every step heavy. One, two, three, eight, ten numbers in my head, maybe not numbers, maybe a time, a place or—a memory. I don't need to wake her up but I want her to wake up. I make a noise as I climb the last step, the bedroom seems dark. I walk over to her restful sleeping figure. She opens her eyes as I pull the covers over her. She must have felt the warmth of the cover on her bare arms, the heat of the duvet on her body.

She looks at me with love and adoration. Then something changes, her eyes are open wider, she's blinking less, focused on my face. She tries to get up but I stop her, I bring my large frame to its full six feet length. I quickly look at the exit, the bedroom door she looks to, as if she can read my mind. Does she know what my next move is? She is playing with me, taunting me, daring me to make a move so she can plan her escape, but I'm too quick for her. She tries to get up. I feel the thudding of her heart on my chest, pounding in my ears, vibrating.

I stop her and give her that look that says, "Don't—please don't; I don't want to hurt you, lay still my love, my darling."

I take my eyes off her to look at the clock—the clock—something in the back of my head. What has the clock got to do with how I feel? The hands of a clock back to back. What does that even mean.

She makes her move. She is down the stairs before I can stop her, counting them as she goes, always counting one, two, three, seven, nine. There are 13.

Don't turn around. I am right behind you; step for step. She is looking for her keys, she looks scared as she looks up at the stairs. I have hidden them, I chuckle a throaty demonic sound. She finds them, and she is out of the front door as I reach it. She reverses off the drive and into the cold dark night. The cold air hits me and cuts into me like icicles stabbing my body. I should have put on a T-shirt; my feet are cold. Where are my shoes? I try to scream but there is no sound, just my frosty breathe in the cold night air.

I unlock the car and slide into the seat. I am not sure what is happening, he is watching me, and quickly reverse off the drive. I can see him in the door way, his large frame covering any light from inside the house. He is walking, running. I don't know. My mind is going into overdrive. I don't know what's real any more. What has happened to my loving and caring husband? Who has done this to him? Why is he trying to hurt me? I look in my rear-view mirror. I cannot see him. I let out a sigh of relief.

I remember when we first met, memories; tears, laughter happy and sad times. We never had children. Whose choice was that? Why did we never have children? I wanted them. Did he not want children? I look again and my heart beats faster. I can see his car and he is driving fast. Got to keep going faster and faster. I don't look any more, but instead I stop the car. He has been having bad dreams for a while now, could that have affected him? I noticed how he calls out names, warning them. Who is them? Mark, Dean, Danny, Jess. Friends from school? Did something happen to them? Is that why he is acting this way? I feel the cold now even more.

I start the car up. Where am I going? I want to go to the safeness of my home, the warmth of my husband's arms, to smell the scent of his smell on his body and feel his breath on my face, neck and body. But then I remember the twisted look on his troubled face, the look of insanity like he wants to sink his white pearly teeth into my flesh, but more so, I remember the blood around his mouth and his teeth.

I look in the mirror to see where he is. Not far behind me the car is swerving.

My hands are clawing at the doorway as I try and restrain myself. I want to follow her. Why does my chest hurt so much? Like I've been punched. I reach up to calm myself, my hand brushes a scar close to my heart, where she is too.

I remember when we first met. It was love at first sight. This vision of beauty standing with friends in the market square under the big clock. Her hair flowing behind her as the wind caught it and whispered things in her ear only she could hear. Her laugh infectious. The way she turned graciously. She stopped and looked at me, gave me a friendly smile. We became an item, and it was wonderful. Every day full of surprises; no day the same. She reminds me of someone I knew a long time ago…why can't I remember. I need to go after her, I need to say, "Sorry, JESS!!!"

A scream escapes from deep within my throat. I need you. I am confused. Who is Jess? Why would I say that name? I remember a girl a long time ago, a girl I dearly loved. Memories running, running away. My head is cloudy and heavy, and it hurts badly.

My nostrils flare as the smell of her perfume lingers in the car, and fills my head. I need her now. I sniff the air. It smells like winter, Christmas stews—pollution and snow.

WHERE IS SHE? Sophie!!! The little red mini with a white heart on the side. She loved this little car so much. I remember the day she saw it. She was so excited, jumping up and down, clapping her hands, her eyes sparkling. A car we went everywhere to find. We went almost everywhere together, and now it is the only way she can escape me. She sees me and stops; I speed up to catch her. The car is spinning, and I cannot control it; then darkness covers me, and the feeling of sinking fills me.

*****

Chapter 9

There was sound coming from somewhere—a siren, as a police car zoomed past. Sophie sat there waiting, her heart was slower than usual as if her body was trying to will time to slow down; for life to stop right at that moment. She could hear everyone downstairs, closing doors, and switching on the TV.

The news, breaking news blaring from the TV. She could hear the voice of the news caster; something must've happened. It was dark and calm outside. The moon was full and frightening; this is when he was the strongest. Sophie shook as he crept into her mind. He was lovely, kind and sweet until something changed. He would stare at her, he looked stronger, and he was a stranger.

She shook her head. He was dead. She had seen his car go over the edge. She had seen him.

The phone started beeping; the alarm's two minutes were up. The box was lying on its side as she collapsed on the floor, her heart wanted to stop as another's started beating.

Chapter 10

I'm OK. I can move but the pain shoots up my neck. Memories flood back as the smoke rises. My claws scratch at the paint, pushing the door wide for me to fall out. The sirens blare. The police officer looks like Danny. I push past him. I need to go home.

"Sorry sir, please step back." He's pushing me away. There's smoke coming from nearby. I can't see where it's coming from. It must be nearby.

"Sir, I'm sorry. There's been a fatality."

My heart stops.

"Sophie."

Chapter 11

I travelled by car to avoid human contact. My car was written off. The rest was a blur. The insurance company delivered something, stopping only when the car was out of gas. Eventually I was home, my real home. It looked familiar and safe; it was where I grew up. Memories flooded my eyes. In a loving environment; my parents. An ache hit my chest. They had died a long time ago it seemed. The house was overrun with weeds and the trees had fallen. Mum, my kind, loving, beautiful mother and my dad. It was too much.

The old place looked the same, the roof needed attending to, but it had no holes, I sat on the steps eyeing where it had all begun. I feared nothing anymore. There was nothing to lose. It stood there, the entrance to my own hell. The barn had not fallen but fell so many.

I clenched my fist and dropped to the ground. I was running towards the barn. It creaked as I ran through the heavy doors. They moved so quickly with my force, this pleased me. I sat their empty, frozen in time. No remnants of the creature that had infected me. Nothing to show what had happened since I'd left. It had frozen; life here had frozen. The sun was hot. I fiddled with the taps to turn on the shower. Cool water neutralised the beast that kept rising up. I stood under there for hours trying not to reminisce.

As I got out, the memories did not stop. Memories of how we stood back to back. How I killed Jess, her hot flesh falling to the floor. My blood boiled, and I shuddered. Deep within me something rose, and I let out a howl and fell to the ground shaking.

I stayed there for a while thinking, regretting. Time is meant to polish memories but mine were as dull as ever. What if I didn't go into the barn that day? What if I told them that I had been bitten? Would I still be here?

Would I have met Sophie?

I wince thinking of her. I was happy; we met and fell in love. Laughing all the time. She would laugh at my strength as I would scoop her up. Now she feared me. The strength came first; I noticed when I lifted the sofa with one hand shortly followed my sense of smell, then acute hearing, then nails like daggers, and finally the need to hunt. Something I couldn't shake.

All that was the past, it is all what ifs. My thoughts turned to Edie. I had taken the path where she had once lived and thrived. I had walked down the path she had walked down. Had I been tracking my prey? Until I found her. I had seen the light drain out of her eyes, when I had bitten into her slender pale neck. I turned to leave the barn, afraid to have my back to it but strong enough to do it. I walked slowly, building up pace until I reached the lake opposite the school.

The town had not changed. A population of 1,000 invisible people. I made my way to the janitor's shed, our spot. I had hated it here; all dust and tools, it had not changed. The hinges on the door hung loosely, swinging the door all the way back. The ceiling with its patch of damp dripping relentlessly on the tools beneath it, rusting them as it fell. As I turned to leave, it caught me, beneath the windowsill; a jacket. I knew this jacket. I walked towards it slow and weary until I caught his scent. Mark. It flooded my every sense, flaring my nostrils dilating my pupils. I was almost dizzy with excitement. I'm hungry. I left immediately, carrying the jacket, refreshing myself with the scent every few minutes.

I stopped instantly, transfixed by the asylum. Standing tall and dark, bars on the windows and wire across the tops of the gates. The cave of the madman—like attracts like, I guess. I was always afraid of this place but now it made me curious. I approached the gates, feeling the cool bars under my hands. It was not scary, it was oddly beautiful—a cage. I was so in awe of the building that I almost did not hear the voices. I hid behind the wall.

It was Dean; he was in the courtyard playing with a little blonde curly haired girl about 5 years old running jumping and climbing. She was calling for her daddy to chase her. I couldn't help but stare, it was him. My friend, my brother. A pang of jealousy hit me, anger bubbled up inside.

I should have been happy, like this with Sophie. I should have had a family, I deserved it. I had been hurt, I had lost everything. I spied on them a bit longer, through the wrought iron gates, keeping out of sight. Dean looked old and troubled, but still kept his good looks. He looked like a man who had been through a war and survived.

Danny came out next, all grown up and, Mark, he looked the same. Two women and three more children came out to enjoy the sunshine. Seeing Mark jolted me back from the scene I was watching. I was still holding his jacket which I threw to the ground. They had moved on, not tried to find me or save me. I was angry, I leant back and let out a silent howl from deep within me.

Looking up at the sky I suddenly realised there was silence in the air, no birds singing, no crickets, no nothing. Even the leaves on the trees stopped moving as if time stood still. Joe wasn't the only one who had noticed, if he had looked through the gate he would have seen Dean stop and look up. Mark gathered the women and children up, and moved them inside quickly and quietly. I came back to reality and looked through the gates. Nobody was in the courtyard anymore, where had they gone. I reached up to the bars, to try to climb over but it was too high.

Dean and Danny looked towards Mark. They were already on it; they had been waiting for this day to come for a very long time. They had followed the stories in the newspapers about Joe, about the accident. They had hoped that would have been his end. They read about the kitten, about the young girl who was found in the forest with no face, and about his beloved wife Sophie.

They had spied Joe outside the gates watching them as they walked out. They were ready for him and had been for a long time. Dean looked through the big telescope and saw Joe trying to climb over the big strong wrought iron gates, the ones he prayed would not let this demon in.

Joe was getting angrier and angrier, the sun beating down on him. He looked like he was snarling, biting, jumping, and clawing at the air wishing he could fly but there was no way to get within these walls of this great compound. He ran up and around the compound, back and forth, up and down frothing at the mouth twitching and howling like a banshee.

Then he stopped. Dean watched as Joe turned to face him as if he knew he was watching. Staring dead at him, Joe grinned and bared his teeth.

Dean was scared for his family, for his brothers, and for the team who resided in this asylum. Joe ran fast hiding and ducking. As the sun got hotter it beat down on Joe; on his back, head and face. His anger engulfed him. Dean looked away as Mark confirmed that the women and children had been taken to safety.

Chapter 12

I stopped running. Taunting Dean was like playing with my food. The thought of them cowering made the adrenaline burn through my every pore. I stopped suddenly as I saw something that made me excited. There was a small dug out crawl space below the wall that encased this big compound. It was so small the human eye would have missed it but not my animal instincts. I found my way in.

I couldn't help grinning. I started digging at the under growth, ripping up clumps of grass and dirt with my bare bleeding hands; panting as I worked frothing at the mouth. I wiped the froth away with my hand and accidently caught my face. I ripped the corner of my mouth without realising my own strength. The blood spilled out running down my arm. It was amazing, glistening as it travelled. I was in awe as it ran to my hands, down my fingers to my nails thickened and sharp. I carried on digging, sizing up the hole, forcing myself into the space, struggling relentlessly until I fell back. I needed to eat. They weren't going anywhere, I needed something, I searched around there was nothing but houses.

On the other side of the wall towards the gate, stood the biggest house. I don't know why I chose this one but maybe I felt like fine dining. With its vast acres of land, the house shone in the sun, the shadows of the trees reflecting on the walls as they danced across the big windows. The solid wood doors with their detailed engraving, like silhouetting ballet dancers pirouetting across a dance floor.

I smiled, which in the reflection of the glass looked like a grimace. My scraggy hair and dirty clothes looked unbecoming. I needed to wash up if I was going to meet my brothers. I made my way to the back of the house, the door was unlocked and I entered into the kitchen. Thinking about how close they were I almost forgot how hungry I was. The house was empty and every footfall echoed against the marble floor. I went over to the refrigerator and pulled at the doors. Who lived here? Their scent was faint; they had not been home for a while.

The fridge almost empty, just bottles of water and something wrapped up tightly. I pulled the freezer door, this was packed. I reached for the first thing I saw, it was a chunk of meat. Heavy and cold, I instinctively bit into it and howled.

It tasted of ice, it was not the warm flesh I craved. It made me angry, not satisfying an ounce of my hunger. I threw it at the wall and opened the fridge door. The tightly wrapped package was on the bottom shelf, I grabbed it frantically. I was famished, it was some cooked chicken which I ravaged bones and all. If only someone came home. Sophie would have loved it here. I feel a familiar pang in my heart. I had to finish my past so I could build my future with her.

I would find her, but for now, with my hand dripping I bring back my focus. It wasn't until I stepped back to look at it in all its glory that I felt some relief. On the white wall with my blood, 15:37. I let out a loud hoarse inhumane, laugh it echoed around the kitchen and around the big house.

Some species hunt for pleasure not just need, he'd seen this on the discovery channel with his dad. Mum would cringe and cower behind a cushion as killer whales would leap up to attack seals on rocks. I used to watch Mum, so kind she would not hurt a fly. I spent weekends hunting with Dad, sitting for hours I could hear and smell the deer before the bullet hit it. It was in my blood.

The blood stains on my hand glisten as the light hit them, tracing my hands across the cold walls. There was a dull ache behind my eyes, I couldn't remember the last time I had closed my eyes. I didn't blink anymore.

I pulled myself towards the stairs, someone was in here. The buzzing wouldn't stop, the phone was in her pocket caught between the remains of her coat and her jeans. The space was too tight to reach into the pocket without standing. Her heartbeat was in her ears, breathing shallow. This wasn't what her life was meant to be like. She heard his steps as he walked past, they were heavy echoed like a march; more than one person. What was in him? She had caught his reflection in the mirror whilst at the top of the stairs. His laugh had alerted her and then she saw 15:37 sprawled in blood. Who was he? Her stomach was tight and heavy, the vibration in her jacket stopped and so did he.

Chapter 13

Danny heard it first, the howl from hell. The fright bought him to his knees, praying for this not to be true. Mark came running into the room with Dean on his heels. "How did he get in?" Mark asked. Nobody said anything they just stared at each other. Quickly prepared for the worse, they moved quickly and quietly. A cry from the dining room got them to their feet and running. The women and children were safe. Joe would never find them. They had prepared a long time ago, made rooms that were not easy to find and were sound proof. This was the others; they were shouting, screaming, fear on faces as if there were a hundred demons inside the complex.

"GET THE DART GUN QUICKLY!!!" shouted Dean.

Mark ran into the corridor then stopped, frozen to the spot.

Joe was standing there waiting. "Hello Mark," Joe said. He spoke quietly with a hint of a cackle, froth and bubbles forming on the corners of his mouth.

Mark tried to call for help but no sound came out of his mouth, he found his feet and stepped back slowly one step at a time, Dean and Danny stepped out into the corridor and froze. Mark stepping backwards, Joe leaning up against the wall like he was taunting them. He didn't fear their dart gun, he feared nothing. Mark wasn't fast enough and he knew that.

Searching from side to side with his eyes for something heavy to throw at him, to injure him or slow him down.

Joe looked dishevelled and shorter, more hunched like a tiger when it is close enough to sprint before leaping onto its prey.

Joe jumped high, it was inhumane. Instinctively they all ran back to the room from which they had come. The door had heavy bolts and would buy them some time. As Mark turned to run he tripped, falling heavily onto the floor. Dean and Danny were back in the room before they realised that Mark was not with them. Without hesitation they ran back to get him. This was their pact.

Mark lay there preparing for death, for the weight of Joes body on him and the impending darkness. Hopefully he had given Dean and Danny time to escape. Time was slowing down. Mark flinched as he looked around. Joe had stopped in mid—air then landed on his feet looking around. He appeared transfixed on the corner of the room, smiling and sighing to himself.

Chapter 14

I can't believe what I was seeing. There in the dark corner was a shape, forming before my eyes, a foggy apparition. A figure of a girl, she was faint and unsteady but it was her, it was JESS! The joy I felt was indescribable. I felt almost human. I couldn't see anything else but her, and she gave me smile an almost human smile. The growl had gone, it was her, it was JESS—JESS.

"Is that you?"

She didn't reply but I knew it was her with her long hair and bright eyes. She was looking down but it was her. It was as if my entire being was taunting me, my conscience had the better of me. I reached out to her and caught sight of my hand—reality struck me. As suddenly as she had appeared she disappeared. I couldn't breathe. Mark was gone.

Chapter 15

He relayed to them what he had seen. They didn't believe him obviously as Jess was dead. They knew, Joe was psychotic that's why he had been calling out her name. Driven mad with guilt. There was a dead eerie silence in the corridor and in the house, it seemed bigger than before but with nowhere to hide. They had to become the hunters if they were to ever be free of him and his hell. They emerged from the room slowly, the corridor was clear. There were weapons hidden in every room that needed to be gathered. In the far end of the corridor, in a corner tucked away deep in the dark, Joe stood watching and waiting.

The men made it to the rooms at the farthest part of the building without encountering Joe, wondering at every turn where he was. The silence was broken like glass, with mayhem; shouting, screaming, laughing, thuds and bone cracking. The men ran along the corridor turning into the next winding corridor. What they saw was too evil for their eyes. Blood splattered up the walls, droplets clawing their way down the flowered wallpaper like they were in a race. Like hands trying to reach the floor seeing who can get there first. It was everywhere, the smell made Dean feel light headed.

The laughing moved them from the horror, it came from the man they once knew. Who had the heart of a saint, tears fell from their eyes and sadness enveloped them like fog. He needed to die.

Noise interrupted their thoughts, the three men looked up weapons raised and ran towards it. A figure appeared from the big open front door. Someone had hidden, someone had survived. It was Matt, he helped in the kitchen; a kind and gentle giant who was now shaking uncontrollably. He stayed on the floor cowering from the monster who had destroyed his life. Everyone was gone.

The guys followed the noises, he must have hidden. Back to back together as always they scoured each room, opening each door and looked at each crevice. Where had he gone?

Chapter 16

Exercise is important especially after a big meal. I managed to step out, looking around hoping to catch a glimpse of my brothers—playing with my food. Star jumps were fun, so was running. I momentarily slip into a memory of us playing football which I quickly shake away. I feel so good, energy coursing through my veins. I feel like I could sprint faster than Bolt, I'm sure I can. I am the blur. I am flash. I am also not as funny as I think. I chuckle and slip back into a memory of her. Sophie thought I was. Her laugh; I miss her laugh.

They're outside now at the back of the house, I can hear them. I slam the door hard so they hear it, laughing as I lock it. It was time for them to come to me.

Chapter 17

The door slammed and they flinched as they heard the lock turn. He's inside and so were they. If he had found the workers, he'd find the families too. They had factored in his ability to smell but not his speed. His strength, but not his insatiable hunger. He had gained all this but not lost his mind. He was thinking, calculating and hunting them. This was what scared them the most.

The night was drawing in and they had to get back into the house. They had to think of a plan to trap Joe before he attacked again. There was the goods entrance that led to the basement at the side of the building for storing dried goods. Danny's claustrophobia loomed over him. The entrance was small and so was he. The only one who could use this to get back in and unlock the front door for them to get in.

Dean looked at each other and him. They knew his fear, his aversion to lifts, his rapid breathing as he stared at the entrance. It wasn't just the thought of the abyss which loomed beyond this hole that bothered Danny, but the faint reflection in the windows above. He was watching them.

Mark reached out and squeezed Danny's shoulder, pulling him back and leading them away from the building.

The plan was to slowly and gradually prise Joe out of hiding. He needed to be away from the entrance of the basement to give Danny any chance of making it inside. They had to lure him out.

Dean stood up and looked at them, staring down at the floor plans of the building. The longer he was inside alone, the more time he had to find their families. He felt a lump grow inside his throat which he swallowed down. He reached into his pocket, the knife glinting in the sunlight. A smooth strike across his palm. Mark and Danny leapt up.

"What have you done?"

Chapter 18

My nostrils flared, the scent filling every crevice. I shook violently, almost falling to the ground. I knew that scent. I needed to get to it. I ran to the nearest window, they were no longer in the yard. Where had they gone?

Chapter 19

Danny was first to put his hand up at the plan. Dean and Mark looked at him with admiration and a sense of dread. Danny wasn't the fastest or the bravest but he had compassion and with that gift, he could accomplish anything. The three friends made their way to the cellar, in and out of the bushes they darted, they stopped breathing heavily. Adrenaline pumping around their bodies, fear of being sited. The entrance wasn't large but big enough for Danny to squeeze down. The men hugged each other as if their lives depended on it. Praying silently, Mark and Dean lowered Danny down the hole, the blue bulbous veins protruded from foreheads as they bent forward, struggling not to drop him with a thud.

Danny had never been in the basement before; the light from the small bulbs was dim he could just make out what was in front of him. He felt blind, careful to make no noise, he took of his shoes and held them in his hand. It took him a while to find the stairs leading up to the main corridor. As he got to the top of the stairs a noise startled him. He looked around to make sure no one was with him. Mark and Dean's shadows were no longer visible; he was alone. Eyes wide open as he peered to the top of the stairs, he could hear talking. Muttering, and throaty noises.

As he crept up and looked through the crack in the door he could see Joe talking to himself. Pulling at his hair, clawing ears, eyes blood shot, frothy spit around his mouth mixed with blood. Then Joe stopped as if he heard something. Danny felt his heart start beating fast and loudly. He could feel his heart thumping against his chest, willing it to stop. Joe turned slowly looking around grinning from ear to ear making his way towards the cellar door dancing, gliding, and spinning; he moved daintily. Danny stepped back and staggered, he grabbed the stair railings.

Chapter 20

I couldn't focus, the smell of his blood was driving me insane. I needed to get to it but another's scent was pulling me in the opposite direction. I was caught in frustrating excitement. Blood, it was enthralling me with its potency, it was close by and then far away. Although there was also a familiar warm scent coming from the basement, a slow creeping sound up the stairs towards me. It was funny that they didn't know I could sense them. No matter where they went I would always find them.

Chapter 21

A loud sound; it sounded like fireworks. Danny pulled himself up and crept up to the door again, looking through the crack. Joe wasn't there, he had gone. Danny stealthily crept across the first-floor corridor, silently praying and hoping he was alone. Holding his breath as he reached the window, pulling it upwards to release the catch and give them a way in. The slight breeze hit Danny's forehead as the sweat raced down his brow. Careful not to let it fall anywhere and his scent to be marked, he quickly wiped it away with his sleeve and ran. Danny followed the sound of the fireworks out into the foyer and into the kitchen to hide.

Mark and Dean were there, letting off fireworks; hoping that the noise would frighten Joe or at least buy Danny some time. It was unnerving that Joe had not come flying into the foyer like a wounded wild beast. He was there, they knew, every now and then they could swear they could hear him laughing. They needed to find Danny. Mark and Dean sprinted fast towards the cellar, as the haze caused by the fireworks offered a smoke screen. Down they both went, into the darkness hoping Danny was there and safe. Afraid to call out his name, they raced down the steps. The door shut quickly behind them. Dean froze, all he could see was the quick eyes reflecting the dim light, as the beast was on all fours racing towards them.

Joe flew down the cellar stairs and stood opposite the two men, standing up straight to his full height, the two men thought he looked taller and broader. He looked scary but not scared. It was the first time that they had seen him up close, eyes red, a wild look on his face, a lop-sided toothy grin where he had lost part of himself. He wasn't the man they knew. Without warning Joe lifted up his arms and flew at the men. Dean and Mark stepped back in fright and surprise. Joe fell through the boards, down into a crevice with a loud piercing scream. A big dust cloud filled the basement the two men looked down in amazement to see their friend on the ground. His eyes closed and he wasn't moving. This wasn't how it was meant to be. They felt a wave of sadness, and relief was over them as they moved a board over their friend's final resting place. They would bury him properly they agreed, somewhere where he would find the peace that he needed. Firstly, they needed to evacuate the building and find Danny. They felt their stomachs drop thinking about Danny. They prayed he was alive.

Danny had not realised how small a space could feel, his claustrophobia was intense. As he hid in the small pantry he feared Joe would join him. What if Dean's scent was not enough for him? What if he had already gotten to Mark and Dean? His breathing started to quicken as he felt panic wash over him.

Chapter 22

I was not happy. I picked myself off the floor. I didn't feel pain anymore, which was good, as I popped my knee back into place. My arm didn't look right either, it looked lower and if I could feel pain I would have screamed. I ran holding it in place to the wall, the noise as it popped back into place echoed up from my hell.

It was cold and damp. I couldn't make out what this place was. I reached to try to climb up the walls, the slippery walls meant I got so far and fell backwards. The frustration fast became anger, I will destroy them. Clambering and hitting each stone, I felt the anger burn me, I let out a howl deep from within me, a wave of red heat over my eyes.

Chapter 23

Danny could not breath. He was hyperventilating as they opened the pantry door and he fell to the ground in a delirious state. He was saying something that they couldn't make out; something about his eyes. Someone's got a gun? They pulled him to the wall and tried to help him breath. He was shivering between consciousness. They sat with him as he drifted into his exhaustion. Their friend needed to rest.

Everybody in the house celebrated that night, glad they could come out of hiding. Happy that Joe was gone, celebrations were a plenty. Wine flowed and the children played, happy and contented. Mark, Dean and Danny stood in the corner watching them, not feeling the unease that they could see in the eyes of their families and friends. Lost that society beyond these walls did not know the beast in the basement, who would have terrorised them.

Deans hand hurt, the bandages soaked in blood hidden in his pocket. Marks body ached and Danny's eyes glazed with tears. Finally, some peace.

A few months went by and the household went about its daily duties. Men fixing outer buildings and mending. Women cooking, and sewing with small children at their feet. The older children playing. Animals basking in the glorious sunshine; everybody was happy. The wrought iron gates of the asylum glistened in the sunlight, lizards climbing the hot black metal decorative structure.

Chapter 24

I could hear the celebrations fade as time went on, knowing they were for me. I grinned, I snarled and I planned; my facial features stuck like glue. I couldn't tell day from night, there was no light here. I was left in this pit of fury, they had condemned me to hell. Where was the pity for their brother, they left me for dead. I stood up, squinted my eyes. I had to use my senses, feel the surroundings. I started picking at the clay, salt and cement to loosen bricks to make steps. The clay and cement were hard, compacted and painful to dig out. My fingers bled but I was oblivious to it.

Nobody thought of me, nobody remembered me. I was in their past, they thought I was dead, that they had killed me. I spent the days in anger, clawing my way from nightmare to reality; and the nights whimpering in memory of my life before. Jess, Sophia, my friends, my school and my life.

My whimpering echoed further than I knew. They drew her towards me, she remembered me. I lured her to me daily, she was feeding me, giving me water and talking to me. My saviour felt pity for me, she was not strong enough to lift me but I was strong enough to bring her to me.

Chapter 25

They decided to bury him deep in the forest amongst the trees, flowers and the flowing brook. Its peaceful surroundings were ideal. Not one of them wanted to go into that cellar and had not been. With the smell of death, they had put it off for a while now, but it was time. They left it until the evening when everyone was in bed, one by one they went in the cellar, surprisingly it didn't smell of death maybe the salt from the walls preserved the body they thought.

Dean was the first to clear the top of the hole with a hammer in his hand. Mark took out the nails and with anticipation, the three of them; they lifted off the cover very slowly. It was too dark to see anything. Danny flicked on a flashlight, shining it into the gap.

Chapter 26

A lot of back packing travellers had arrived. Their coach broken down in front of the building, they begged for help as the rain poured without relent. Reluctantly they were all given rooms for a couple of nights before they became permanent residents. They were pleasant and started the celebrations. The drunken young men sung merrily, clinking glasses and laughing loudly. The women helped bring a new wave of laughter to the place. Their lives became their business; the place buzzed and took on new life. They were so caught up in the growth and future that they didn't notice.

Tory was the eldest of the girls. She kept the younger ones in line, she herself wandered around looking at the big portraits of ladies of years ago; with their elaborate long fancy dresses, they must have been very hot and sweaty, she thought as a little smile danced upon her lips. The gentlemen with their long white beards. She was impressed, she liked art and would have liked to become an artist but her parents were very ill and they could not afford for her to go to art school. So she gave up school to look after them both, she still liked to sketch, which she did most elegantly. Tory was tall and slender for her 20 years of age. She wasn't of great beauty; a plain scrawny girl but beautiful in her own way, she was kind and loving.

She came across the half open cellar door and stepped down into the darkness. She had often thought she could hear a noise, a cry for help late at night as she walked past before bed. Today she had decided to investigate. She reached for the light switch, her heart was beating quickly. She had not been here before and was a little anxious. All the horror films she'd ever seen had warned her not to go into the basement, but common sense was not so common it appeared. She ignored all her fight or flight instincts. She must have had a little too much drink, as she turned, she heard it again, a whimper.

An animal must be hurt, clearly it was coming from underground, and she scrambled around the floor kicking newspapers, dirt and dust until she came across a raised floorboard. It was nailed to the ground but there were gaps on the sides. She clambered to the floor to peer down the hole. It was dark and there was a strong metallic odour coming from there. Her eyes met his and she fell backwards. That was not an animal. She scoured around until she felt something heavy in her hand, trying to use all her strength to pull out the nails. He was whimpering. The poor man was clearly unwell. She managed to move one side of the board, praying it was enough space for him to climb out. It was not, she called out to him.

Tory couldn't make out what it was; an animal, a man or a monster. Nevertheless, it looked emaciated and dirty. The smell was of death; an acrid smell which burnt your eyes and hurt your nose. He spoke softly, he spoke of entrapment and of devilment, of being betrayed by his brothers. He asked but little of Tory a drink, some food, which she obliged. He asked to not tell anyone of this meeting, he wanted her to trust him and she wanted to be loved and wanted.

Chapter 27

The cover lifted. The bent nails were difficult to put out. The smell of dead flesh hit the three men with a vengeance, they knew he was dead and stopped for a moment to remember their beloved brother, friend and companion; heads bent in union and prayer.

The three men looked in the space, the light darting side to side. Up and down. Joe was gone. They spied a ladder. They all stepped back and looked around them. Frightened and scared, they made a run for the cellar door; tripping up on each other trying to get out first, they locked the door when they got on the other side. They looked at each other in horror, he was gone. Danny fell to the ground, and Dean began to sweat. The people, they had to warn them, they were in danger. The three men separated. Through the day, their loved ones were once again behind closed doors, locked up to keep them safe. The backpackers were told there was a dangerous beast on the prowl and to stay in their rooms until it was caught, the fear and horror of the day took its toll on the men. They huddled together trying to figure out what to do.

Fog erupted in the dark. In a corner of the main corridor, it escalated through the house until it came to a stop by the room the friends were in. It stopped outside the door, then slid underneath it; the men did not notice it until it covered half of the room. They stood still like statues bathed in the moon light as it shone through the windows. They started coughing and felt faint. He was still in the house and he was healing fast, they would not get the chance to plan, he had already started the battle.

Chapter 28

Tory helped Joe out of the well after a week of talking to him, every chance she got. With a ladder, she snuck down from the pantry. It was small and wooden but thin enough to slip through the gap. She was shocked by his appearance but said nothing.

He snarled and grunted as he climbed out of the well, like a frail animal. He reached the top and clambered out on all fours. He asked her to put the cover back on the well and put the nails back in. She didn't question him, she could not imagine the pain he had felt being trapped. Tory didn't see his affliction, she saw someone who needed help. Tory, dark haired pulled back in a ponytail was an only child, she never dated or was even asked. All her friends were pretty or gorgeous. She decided to go travelling, along the way she made friends, no one special until she met Joe. Joe, who like her was an outcast, she had found her match.

Chapter 29

Tory settled me and brought me food and drink, not the kind I needed but it would do. She brought me warm clothes and wept as she told me my body had lost a lot of muscle and I was very weak.

Only I knew my strength. I needed my new pet. She would be useful. She mirrors me, as I grin, she smiles back, not knowing what I'm thinking. I get her to take me upstairs when she's startled by the furore upstairs. A lot of people are moving out in spades. She doesn't know what's going on when I ask her. She stands up to go to investigate and I grab her hand. Her pulse is quick when I touch her and her cheeks flush pink. She's mine.

Chapter 30

The back packers made their way outside the wrought iron gates; some complaining, a few fine with the situation. They still couldn't understand why they had to leave; who was in danger?

The few that complained, stopped and turned around; they didn't want to leave. They found a way back in, through the side entrance of the house. They found their way to the cellar, the smell was atrocious. An animal or rat must have died and rotted in there. But they had nowhere to go, the smell became a normal smell mingling in with the sawdust and dirt.

A few of the boys went in search of food and drink. They found the kitchen, trying to stay away from the corridors so that they couldn't be made to leave. They didn't catch it at first, walking past it numerous times. It was when they finally went to close the door to the cellar they saw it. What was that written on the wall—15:37.

It was a long way up to the attic, a lot of floors to cover, and corridors. The door to the attic was closed when they got there, a chink of light was visible under the door. A shadow moves back and forth, a shuffling can be heard. The men have no plan, they can only hope Joe is weak and unstable. Joe and Tory are taken by surprise when the men burst in, but Joe is faster than they thought, he jumps up and throws himself at the three men.

Dean stepped back quickly, but Danny and Mark were knocked down. Joe escaped down the stairs and into the house. Tory tries to follow Joe but Dean is quick and tackles her. She screams and scratches his face, her fists flying Mark helps Dean tie Tory up and they escort her downstairs.

Joe hides in the linen cupboard he stays there until night time; sniggering, cackling, frothing, twitching and spitting. His involuntary responses.

The backpackers are so drunk that they fall asleep. They don't hear Joe entering the cellar. His eyes were so wide open, you could see the red veins in his eyes. He cannot believe his luck they can't hear his throaty laugh he looks around and smiles. He can feel the heat from their bodies as they lay next to each other. He has to be quiet and quick, the idea comes fast and quick. He makes out the shapes of three men and two females, he shuffles over to the cover on the ground and rubs his hands together. Excited he does a little jig, and bites his ravaged lips.

Chapter 31

In the dining room, the men have Tory tied up, wondering what they should do.

"Why were you with him? Do you have any idea what he could do to you?" Mark was shouting.

She did not respond, instead kept looking down in anger.

"He will kill you," Mark came close to her face, forcing her to look up.

Dean pulled him back and whispered, "We can use her as bait to flush out Joe."

Mark still blinded by anger pulled away from Dean, back to Tory. "You will get what you deserve."

The plan was to put her in the cellar. He would find her and then they would put him back in the well. They tried to speak quietly but this building hid very few secrets. Tory sat holding her breath, soaking up everything that was said into her worthless brain. She smiled as if she had a plan, biting her lip to prevent her laughing.

Their conversation was interrupted by Tory's sudden jolt, she almost rose from her seat making a gurgling noise, convulsing in her seat. She thrashed and foamed at the mouth as they stared at her, careful not to move. She stopped and fainted in the chair. They all looked at her in surprise and amusement. They had spent time with Tory, she was the quiet one of the group of people that stayed with them. She was also the best at charades and studying drama.

It took all Mark's strength not to applaud the theatrical performance. Danny walked towards Tory's chair and began pulling it towards the cellar for Joe. Tory could not help but speak as she saw the cellar door. She looked up at Danny and smiled. The smile was a sweet sickly smile.

"Joe would never hurt me."

Mark laughed hard, so hard he felt like he would fall to the ground.

"Monsters hunt babe."

This made Tory very angry, she tried to free herself from the chair but the ropes were too tight. The door shut behind her quickly as she was left in the dark at the top of the stairs.

Joe looked around in the dark, his eye sight was perfect, a stirring in the corner, a young girl sits up and rubs her eyes; she look around and puts her head back down. Joe backs into the shadows, he is not ready to confront them. He sits down on the ground and waits. A noise at the door. Joe stands up snarling and growling; with a thud and a scream the door is shut and bolted.

Tory picks herself off the floor and squints, her eyes aren't used to the dark. A shuffle in the corner has her turning around. Then nothing, no warning, no pain, just calm.

Joe giggles and gags big chunks of flesh in his mouth, the sweetness of the blood as it trickles from his mouth to his chin; a feeling he stops and looks down at his victim.

Tory?

Oh well, never mind. She was useful but I guess I will have to find someone else to charm, he sniggers and coughs.

His meal finished, Joe feels tired, he has had a long night he finds a corner and falls asleep. Upstairs the hunt is on to find Joe, the men don't split up as they are wary and worried they will be picked off one by one. They just want a quiet life, they want to be with their families and friends. The men go into hunt mode. They need to get him back to the basement. It's like hunting an alpha, hidden and protected by his beta. They spend hours walking, ducking and setting traps, hoping he has given up and gone. If only.

As the evening draws in, Dean suggests giving up and trying when it is light.

They are all weary and uncertain. This is not how their lives were meant to be. They lock themselves in the dining room as it only has one entrance, which they take turns on watch. The night is mostly silent. Pacing up and down during Mark's watch, he hears a noise outside the door. He wakes up the other two, who are armed with dart guns. They're not as brave as they want to be, creaking the door open they see nothing. Slamming it shut and bolting it down quickly for safety.

Nothing more happens until the morning; screaming, shouting, and pitiful wailing coming from downstairs wakes them. They all run down the corridors, ending up in the foyer. Crying coming from the cellar.

"Tory."

They had forgotten about her. Going towards the cellar door, they can hear more than one person in pain.

"What the hell?" Danny says.

They unbolt the cellar door and what they see is carnage. They all step back and take in the scene. Blood everywhere, covering the floor like newly laid carpet. Danny was ill immediately, the smell is enough to make them all gag.

Distracted, Joe looks up and makes a dash for the door. Instinctively, Mark is too quick for him and slams and bolts it shut. Leaning on it to keep him in, as he bangs against the door, his strength causing the hinges to look like they're becoming loose. Danny and Dean put their backs towards the cellar door too. He was shouting at them to let him out. His voice was disarming; they hadn't heard him speak for so long. This was not how they would stand back to back.

"Let me out!" First a loud snarl, then in a soft voice, the old Joe spoke, "Come on, Danny, it's me."

They hear scratching, like a puppy against the door begging to be let out. Then it goes quiet. So quiet. That frightens them most.

Chapter 32

I hear them, the sirens. They have called the police? It's funny. It was too late for ambulances. I couldn't be caught, not by them, not by anyone. I push with all my might against the door but the floor is slippery. I use my nails to carve a note to them on the door. I pull back and find my way out. I was ecstatic, elated, and happy with blood coursing around my veins, hitting every blood trail in my body. I need to get away from here the sirens are dulling my senses and the moon is coming out. My hair is starting to stand at its ends and my eyes burn. I catch my reflection in the lake, they're red. I feel myself falling to the ground. I remember seeing my brothers who I love dearly, who I would die for standing over me. Someone holding a gun, the blonde guy Matt they called him. Why did he shoot me? What did I do Mark, Danny, Dean— and Jess? I cry out and wait for a response, nothing just emptiness, my voice echoing around getting lost in space.

My eyes open; the light is blinding. I try to lift my hand to cover my face. I can't. There are nurses standing in vigil. I hear her before I drift back into the abyss.

"It's me, Cara."

Am I in heaven or did god think I would be useful in hell?

Time passes slowly. Each day they inject this 'medicine' into me. It hurts but not as much as my loss. She haunts me, the girl from long ago. I close my eyes to her accusing face, the screams frighten away sleep. I don't seem to need it anymore.

I fight my hunger each time the nurse enters the room. She's a small light in the darkness, her manners are gentle. She fears me I can see it in her eyes; the predators only restrained for now she knows, I suppress the chuckle in my throat. I feel my heart rate slow down, something's not right, I can't breathe. The machines are making high-pitched noises.

HELP ME!!!

I try shouting. My voice is drowned out by the machines. I fall deeper into the darkness.

My leg hurts, and what is that smell? It's hurting my nose, my throat, and stinging my eyes.

Where am I?

People shouting, a girl crying.

Sophie…SOPHIE!!!

I try to shout but my throat hurts. I can't see through the smoke and—and—flames.

HELP!

"Sir, are you OK? The police and fire fighters are doing their best to get you out, stay calm."

I hear muffled noises.

"JOE!!! JOE!"

It's Sophie, she is crying. "Are you OK?" she was asking. I try to answer her, but instead I drift off into the darkness once again.

I can hear soft angelic voices whispering. They sound like they are singing. Am I in heaven?

"Joe, Joe," a whisper.

I try to open my eyes. They hurt and feel hot. "Joe, its Sophie, my love." She keeps fading as I blink.

"I am so sorry. Please forgive me," I say to her. My voice is hoarse. My eyes open, and she is gone. She was never there.

The headache is scaring; the pain feels like someone ripping me apart. The medication is long gone from my system, leaving horrible scars imbedded on my mind.

What was happening to me? She walks towards me with her dark hair. The nurse, she has kind eyes and a timid smile. She brings something towards my arm, and I feel everything slip away.

I went into the barn that day. I was attacked, and I never told anyone. We stood back to back, and I still never told; if only. I reach to touch my hurting chest; it is bandaged, the pain is searing. I drift in and out of consciousness, lost in the haze. I can hear birds singing, the wind as it rustles in the trees. I feel like I'm levitating, swaying with the trees. I hear a door open, muffled voices and then a thud as I fall to the ground.

Sobbing. "He's dead!" Dean leans into Mark for support. Danny stood staring at the ground. They couldn't move for disbelief; their friend was gone. Silence fell onto them.

Chapter 33

"He's awake!"

The voice is unfamiliar; it's soft and kind. She reaches to touch me. I snarl. I feel it building up inside me. I am pulled down by my restraints as I jolt up to lunge. I collapse again. I can only whisper 'help' before I'm gone, as a single tear runs down my face.

The journey was long and tedious. More than a week to the rehabilitation centre; no one could tell me what had happened to me. I was guided by memories and flashbacks. I didn't even know if any of it had really happened.

Chapter 34

She's beautiful in the least obvious way; Cara's hair is long and wispy. She's wearing her uniform. Her eyes bright and blue. As the wind blows it into her face, I get her scent. I look away after she smiles at me and I force one back to her, my face hurts as I reach to touch the scar. She's happy, content and starts singing, she gives me the look—I know this means to stop.

Sophie would drive us home before, she was stunning. In everything she did, she was prime. I remember the way she would keep looking at me every now and then. If I moved, she'd jump from her seat, she was scared of me and I loved it. The blood bubbles around my body, my veins hurt from the pressure of the blood rushing, chasing the trail. I have to keep it to myself, the secrets are still there, the hunger is still there. The pulsating vein in my neck is throbbing. I want to laugh out loud. I want to jump up and down and shout with happiness, but I say nothing and hold my breath.

"Pass me the ticket from the glove box, please, Joe."

I reach inside and something nicks my hand. I'm angry; blood is my trigger. I grab the papers and give them to her without looking. My eyes are transfixed on the paper at the bottom of the glove compartment. Those eyes, I know them. I reach towards it entranced and unfold it from the edges.

"Here you go, Joe, hold these," she shoves the permit at me. I suppress my growl and take it from her.

"Sorry it's such as mess in there, there are things in there from years ago."

I can't hear what she's saying, I feel like I'm shaking, holding the paper so tightly but afraid of it tearing. It was her, her eyes, smile and hair. I feel frenzied. It's her, she's happy about something. I can't read the text it's faded. I can't get past how well she looks, she's so youthful.

Cara is calling me to get out of the car but I can't.

"Get out Joe; we're going to be late!"

I can't move as she grabs the paper from me.

"Look at how old this paper is! It's from a year ago. It's nothing interesting, this woman had won a prize."

She opens the door and throws the paper in the back seat; grabbing my arm, she takes me with her. I feel weak as my mind rushes ahead. Where is she? Where has she been? Who is with her? What is she doing? My mind screams at me to stop as I become acutely aware of Cara's words, "Bet she doesn't look this youthful since giving birth."

What were you doing at 15:37 today?

Epilogue

"He's beautiful."

"Can you call a boy that, Mum?"

"Of course you can, Sophie."

I laugh as she smiles at me with her eyes, and furrows her brow. Classic Mum; correct and confused.

"He is pretty amazing, Mum. He learnt to hold his bottle so quickly. Can't hold his neck up but his bottle he can. This boy has Anderson blood, Sophie. He is strong and clever."

I hate it when Mum says this, he has his blood, too. It fills me with dread.

"Are you sure he's OK, Mum?"

"Of course, Sophie. You had so many scans, tests and appointments with some questionable doctors when all you needed was mama's remedies." She laughs again.

"Kids these days don't listen, do they, Jake?"

"Jake's smiling, Sophie!" Mum's ecstatic.

"He laughed at a cracker this morning, Mum."

Mum has been helping me since he was born and before. She set up the vigil for Joe too. She spends all her time with them, only going home to give Dad his dinner.

"See you loveys tomorrow!" she shouts as she puts Jake down.

I walk towards the kitchen to make dinner too.

"OH! Your little claws," my heart stops.

"Mum."

"He really needs mittens love, little scratchy." I walk towards him in his cot, he is reaching up and I sigh with relief at his little hands in his mouth. No claws.

"See you tomorrow, Mum."

"Bye lovey, stinky pants needs seeing too," as she shuts the door.

Classic Mum. "Come on, stinky." I lift him and immediately regret not holding my breath.

Hello baby, hello baby. I love him so much. I hate laying him down. I want him with me all the time. Wondering if I should get a sling. I will carry him with me forever. I live for his little smile, the cute little dimples. I turn as the phone rings, look back and my world collapses.

His eyes, they're red.

The hunt was just beginning.

CPSIA information can be obtained
at www.ICGtesting.com
Printed in the USA
LVHW080755060422
715401LV00016B/738

9 781398 423299